W9-BIS-359

WOOD COULD

BY TIFFANY STONE
ILLUSTRATED BY MIKE LOWERY

DIAL BOOKS
FOR YOUNG READERS

For Annette, who could and would always play pretend when we were kids, and for her mom, Avril, who remembers.
—T.S.

For Susan M.
—M.L.

Dial Books for Young Readers
An imprint of Penguin Random House LLC, New York

First published in the United States of America by Dial Books for Young Readers,
an imprint of Penguin Random House LLC, 2021.

Text copyright © 2021 by Tiffany Stone
Illustrations copyright © 2021 by Mike Lowery

Penguin supports copyright. Copyright fuels creativity,
encourages diverse voices, promotes free speech, and creates a vibrant culture.
Thank you for buying an authorized edition of this book and for complying with
copyright laws by not reproducing, scanning, or distributing
any part of it in any form without permission. You are supporting
writers and allowing Penguin to continue to publish
books for every reader.

Dial and colophon are registered trademarks
of Penguin Random House LLC.

Visit us online at penguinrandomhouse.com.

Library of Congress Cataloging-in-Publication Data is available
Printed in China
ISBN 9780735230811

1 3 5 7 9 10 8 6 4 2

Hand lettering by Mike Lowery
Design by Jasmin Rubero

OH, SHE MEANT HIM.
WOOD <u>COULD</u> BE A UNICORN.

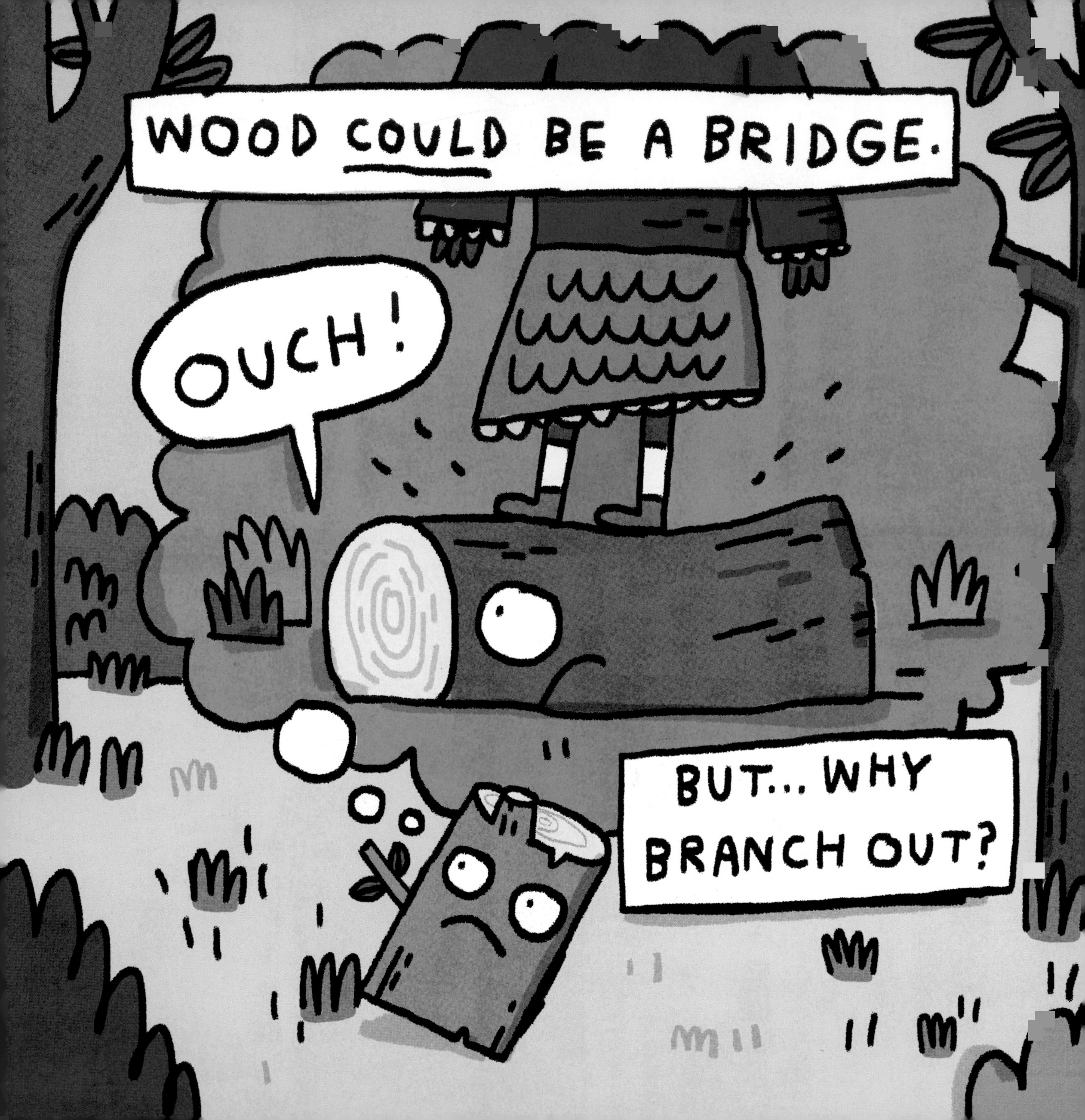
WOOD COULD BE A BRIDGE.
OUCH!
BUT... WHY BRANCH OUT?

PRINCE FLUFFYBUTT'S BEEN KIDNAPPED! PIRATES TOOK HIM AND LEFT HIM ON A DESERT ISLAND! I CAN'T SWIM OUT TO SAVE HIM IN THIS BALL GOWN. IF ONLY I HAD A SHIP. (HINT, HINT.)

BUT...BETTER YET, SHE COULD LEAVE HIM ALONE. (HINT, HINT.)

POP

HE WAS PINING FOR A NAP. WOOD ROLLED AWAY.

FAR, FAR AWAY

WAIT FOR US!

BUT NOT FAR ENOUGH.
HELP! HELP!
A DRAGON FLEW OFF WITH PRINCE FLUFFYBUTT AND DROPPED HIM IN HER NEST. SHE'LL BE BACK SOON AND SHE'S HUNGRY!

BUT... SHE WAS OUT OF HER TREE IF SHE THOUGHT WOOD **WOULD!**

ROLL ROLL ROLL

TAIL UP, PRINCE FLUFFYBUTT. I'LL SAVE YOU!

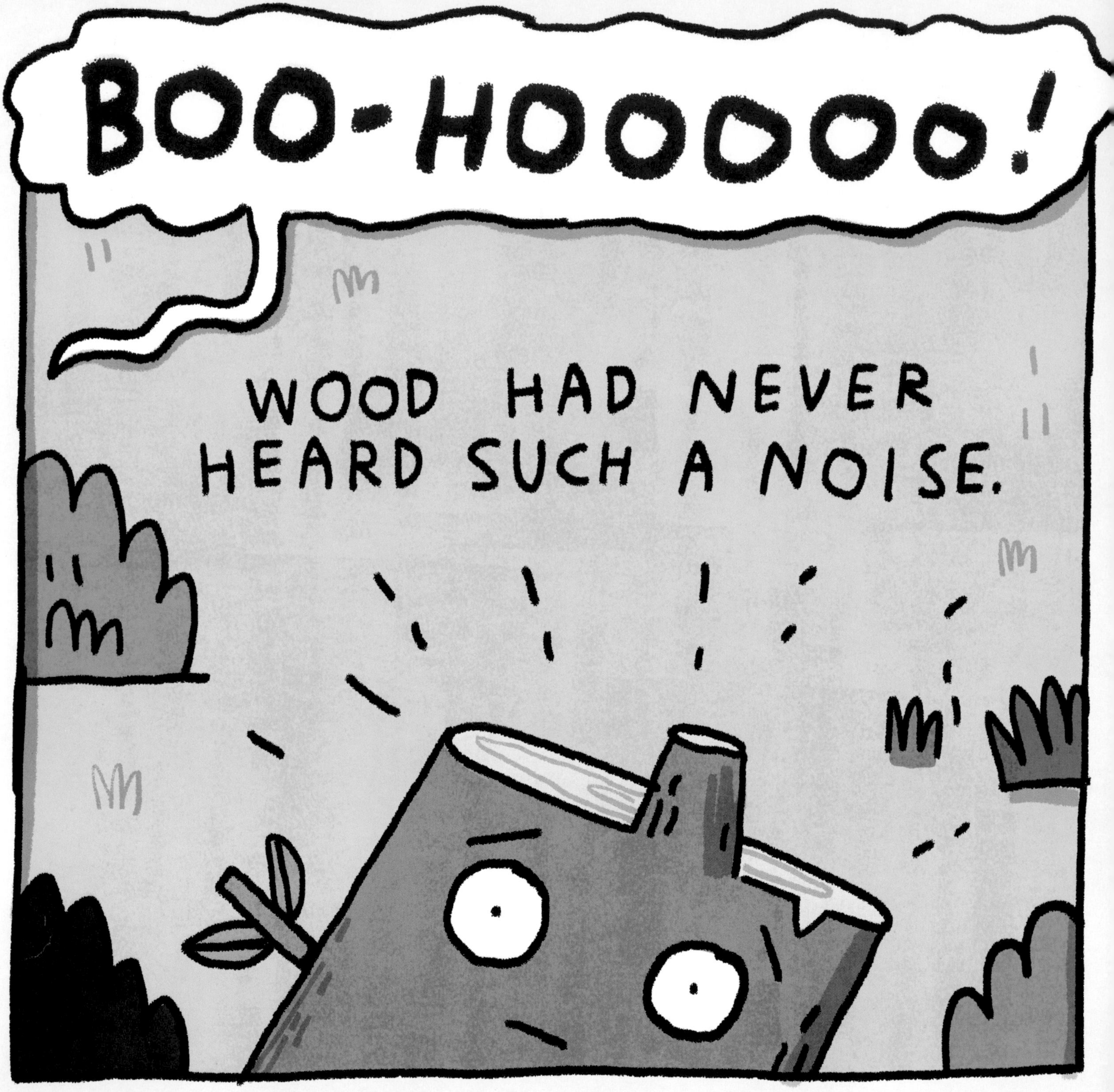
BOO-HOOOOOO!
WOOD HAD NEVER HEARD SUCH A NOISE.

WHAT WOOD FELT WAS BIGGER THAN A SPLINTER.

WOOD FELT A KNOT FORM DEEP INSIDE.

THE KNOT DID NOT FEEL GOOD.

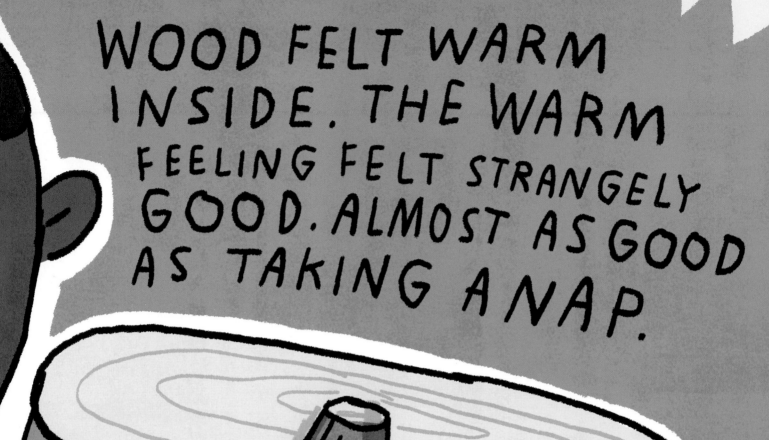

WOOD FELT WARM INSIDE. THE WARM FEELING FELT STRANGELY GOOD. ALMOST AS GOOD AS TAKING A NAP.

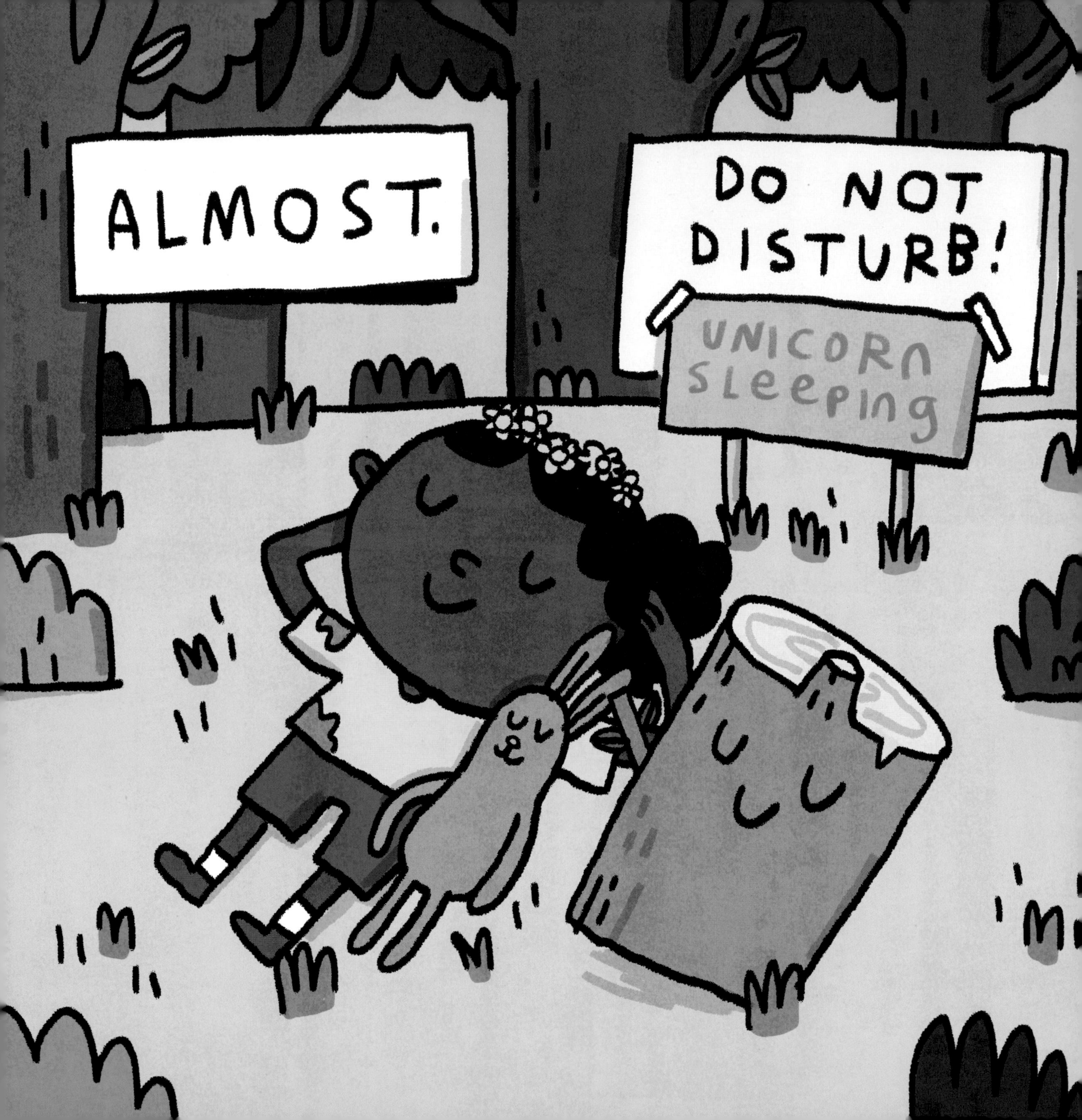
ALMOST.
DO NOT DISTURB!
UNICORN SLEEPING

31192022125528